Liontooth

the story of a garden

Liontooth

the story of a garden

SARA SHARPE

BEAUTIFULBOOKS

First published 2006.

Published by Beautiful Books Limited
117 Sugden Road, London SW11 5ED
www.beautiful-books.co.uk

9 8 7 6 5 4 3 2 1

ISBN 0954947630
ISBN 9780954947637

Printed in the European Community
Design by Ian Roberts
Production by nlAtelier

I'VE ALWAYS LOVED the common names of plants and trees. This story celebrates their extravagance. Re botanical detail I've cheated four times: **Witch** should be **Wych**. **Orchid** is left off **Lady's Slipper**. **Hard Shield** and **Broad Buckler** are ferns. I've made up the **Enchanter with his Nightshade**. The plant is really called **Enchanter's Nightshade**. Otherwise, with the help of the following sources – **Ferguson's Plant Directory** by Nicola Ferguson, **Weeds** by Mary Spiller, **Cottage Garden Flowers** by Margery Fish and **The Wild Garden** by William Robinson – I've tried to be accurate.

THE ILLUSTRATIONS

THE FULL-PAGE PLATES in this book have come from the 1857 edition of **Les Fleurs Animées** by J.J. Grandville (1803-47). Jean Ignace Isidore Gérard, to give him his proper name, began his career in Paris as a magazine illustrator and theatre costume designer. When he was 26, he achieved fame for his **Métamorphoses du jour** which depicted human beings with animal heads. He went on to illustrate Defoe's **Robinson Crusoe**, Cervantes' **Don Quixote** and the works of La Fontaine.

The botanical illustrations are from the 1825 edition of Maund's **Botanic Garden**. Benjamin Maund (1790-1863) was also no ordinary man: he combined the careers of pharmacist, botanist, printer and bookseller, and had a great passion to feed the 19th-century public's fascination with botanical works.

for Cyrano, Winifred, James and Susan Sharpe

with love

CONTENTS

PROLOGUE: *the song inside the helmet*   3

PART ONE: *the coming of discord*   19

PART TWO: *the battle*   51

EPILOGUE: *Dent-de-Lion*   67

APPENDIX I: *postscript*   77

APPENDIX II: *plantings*   81

APPENDIX III: *glossary*   89

the song inside the helmet

NCE UPON A TIME, long long ago, there lived a knight called Liontooth. He was a brave and gentle knight, as brave as his name. His eyes were cornflower blue, his brow broad and high, his smile wonderfully sweet. There were none who met him that did not love him, even those unused to love. Bears lay down like rugs before him. Wizards looked into his eyes and muddled their spells. Villains wept. And since his skill with sword, lance and axe was unrivalled and his quota of dragons slain greater than anyone else's, this knight should have been the happiest of men.

But Liontooth was not happy. Riding in the silence of the honeysuckle woods he had searched his heart and found a hole in it. He was also troubled by a song inside his helmet.

Hoping to fill the hole and quell the song he went abroad and travelled in strange lands. But the hole grew larger and the song louder until, one day, Sir Liontooth could bear it no longer.

'I am an honourable knight,' he cried. *'But all I do is kill. I go to war to uphold what is right, yet, by taking life, I do wrong. Oh lackaday! I am no better than the dragons that I slay!'*

It was afternoon and his eyelids felt like lead. He fell asleep and dreamed of England and a particular hillside facing south and the fat smell of lilac.

And when he awoke, the hole in his heart was gone and its emptiness filled by the most wonderful idea he had ever had. *'I am going to make a garden,'* said Sir Liontooth.

Sir Liontooth began collecting specimens. *'Come and help me make my garden,'* he said to the Snapdragons and they agreed. He called to the Potato Tree in Chile, the Japanese Anemones, the Wisteria in China. A detachment of Mexican Sunflowers, proud as guardsmen, fell in behind him. The Greek Valerians also heard his call. So did the Siberian Wallflowers and the Indian Horse Chestnuts, high in their Himalayan hills.

'Let me come with you,' wailed the Russian Vine, *'before the cruel frost eats my heart.'*

'Certainly,' answered Sir Liontooth, *'but you must sing us your songs.'*

So the Russian Vine joined the company of trees and flowers. Waving his tassels between the Fair Maids of France and the Marvel of Peru, he warbled of winter and slant-eyed horsemen and plains which reach to the end of the world.

After a year Sir Liontooth came home and found, to his delight, another multitude of plants and trees waiting for him. Their leader, the Yellow Archangel, raised his wings.

'Sire, we are here to help you. We have found the particular hillside facing south. Come! Follow us!'

'I want a garden
full of mignonette and lavender
sweet peas and periwinkle
hawthorn and honeysuckle
I want forget-me-nots
and hollyhocks and buttercups
I want a garden of my very very own.'

Sir Liontooth hummed his song and considered his property. Beside him stood his squires, Honesty and Sneezewort. Honesty's doublet was lilac-pink. Bright bobbles bounced on Sneezewort's hat. They were young and gallant and Sir Liontooth loved them. Nearby were his chief advisers: Giant Bellflower, the Witches Elm and Hazel, the Yellow Archangel, the Enchanter with his Nightshade, the Bay Tree, the Elders and a slim elegant person called the Widow Iris.

'That is a most malodorous marsh,' observed Sir Liontooth. *'Let us drain it and make of it a merry meadow.'*

Giant Bellflower rumbled agreement, searched among his bells and made a note in one of them. Then Sir Liontooth made a speech and the trees and flowers and creepers and grasses listened.

'I dream of peace and love,' he said. *'It began with the song inside my helmet, leading me to think that a garden is like music, which, though its parts be as different as Toadflax is from Tarragon,*

Grandville del.   Ch. Geoffroy

Reine Marguerite
Chrisantème.

yet makes of these parts a most harmonious whole.' He paused and turned to Widow Iris. *'Shall we call ourselves the harmonious garden?'* he enquired.

SLOWLY, AMID PLEASURABLE CONFUSION and animated discussion, the harmonious garden took shape. Gardens, like tortoises, cannot be hurried. First Giant Bellflower moved a quantity of earth about, to make curves and sweeps and ups and downs; beds for happy-go-lucky plants; other, more formal beds for dignified, serious flowers; and yet another bed for the cheerful stream which lolloped downhill, dropping in on a few ponds on its way. He drained the marsh and turned it into a merry meadow. He added a lake for the stream to rest in – and round it a loving wilderness for the small, shy things: Mind Your Own Business and Herb Robert and gentle, smelly Wartcress.

Assisting the Giant was Dwarf Reedmace. It was he who suggested a grotto.

'What a fine idea!' cried Sir Liontooth, at his wits' end to know what to do with Fairy Moss and her Mosses whose tempers grew daily shorter. The grotto proved the perfect solution. Now Fairy Moss lay pink with pleasure in her pool, while above her on the rocks the Mosses hung like bats.

'Sire,' rumbled Giant Bellflower. *'Before we proceed further, where is your house to be?'*

Sir Liontooth looked astonished. *'My house?'*

'Gardens always have houses,' said the Giant. *'Always. Where am I to position the great-walled vegetable garden if I don't know where the house is?'*

Sir Liontooth summoned the two Witches and the Enchanter with his Nightshade, told them what he wanted – and suddenly there it was: a small pink chateau with four turrets; a moat full of blue Sweet Peas; between the south-facing turrets a balcony hung on slender pillars which rose to a pale-green roof; a mosque-shaped conservatory; four bridges to cross the moat and arrive in the garden, the north-facing bridge to lead through an arch into the great-walled vegetable garden; with another arch at the north end of the great-walled vegetable garden revealing the foam of a Wild Cherry forest.

Widow Iris, slim and grave, walked among the Lilac and wondered why Sir Liontooth's smile caused a pain in her heart.

IT WAS EARLY ON A SUMMER'S morning six months later. Sir Liontooth awoke and yawned. Then he went out onto his balcony and looked at the garden; a wind ruffled the manes of the Indian Horse Chestnuts; he heard the growl of Dog Rose and saw the soft grey Lamb's Ears prick as a Panther Lily passed.

Jasmine and Lilac, Sweet Pea and Honeysuckle, Moss Rose and
Apple-Blossom caressed him with their scents.

'Not all the perfumes of Araby,' marvelled Sir Liontooth,
'make such a potent beverage.' And he drank in the sweetness,
his head spinning like a weathercock in the north wind.
The garden awoke.

*'Rosemary-hedged, Lavender-edged, where do your paths
lead?'* called Sir Liontooth and young voices answered:

> *'By the Sweet Flag through the Dogwoods*
> *past the Dragons and the Larkspur*
> *past the waving tails of Catmint*
> *where the Creeping Softgrass goes;*
> *down the stream and through the Bracken*
> *to the long-grassed Apple orchards,*
> *to the lakeside's Reeds and Sedges*
> *where the Water Hawthorn grows.'*

'Who sings?' demanded Sir Liontooth, peering through curtains of
Wisteria, twitching back Ivy, lifting the cloak of the Russian Vine asleep in
an ancient tree. Silence, then laughter.

'Come out!' he commanded – and so they did, the five boys and the
seven girls: Ragged Robin, Sweet Basil, Sticky Willie, Creeping Charlie,

Sweet William, Blue-eyed Mary, Black-eyed Susan, Creeping Jenny, Drumstick Primrose, Corkscrew Hazel, Sweet Violet and French Marigold.

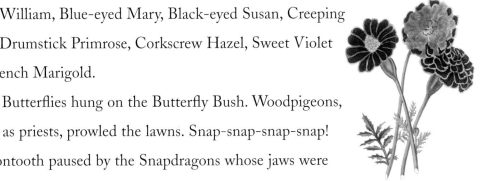

Butterflies hung on the Butterfly Bush. Woodpigeons, plump as priests, prowled the lawns. Snap-snap-snap-snap! Sir Liontooth paused by the Snapdragons whose jaws were never idle. Then he strolled on to the lake and through the loving wilderness where the Elders stood half-asleep in their parliament and the wild pigs Swinecress and Sowthistle rootled in Nettles. He climbed the hillside and looked back through the early morning mist at his harmonious garden and knew – with absolute certainty – that he had never, ever, been so happy.

PART ONE:

the coming of discord

WINTER CAME EARLY and stayed late, wrapping the garden in layers of snow, icing the lake, the grotto, the ponds, thrusting cold fingers into the cracks of the trees. Seemingly dead, the garden slept. Sir Liontooth rode out and about. He sat with old knights, fretful in furs, tilted at icicles and jousted with the north wind.

On Christmas night there was a full moon. Returning home through the forest, Sir Liontooth paused in a clearing to brush the frost from his eyelashes. It was then that he noticed the tree shaped like a woman.

'By my helmet!' he exclaimed. *'It is a woman!'*

She was pale and hardly breathing, bound to the trunk of a Rowan; more a statue than flesh and blood. The snow had blurred her outline, making her one with the tree. Tenderly Sir Liontooth untied the ropes, brushed the snow from her brow and chafed her ice-cold hands and feet. He saw that she was beautiful, with hair dark as a raven's wing and alabaster skin.

'Beauty left for bears!' he cried. *'What wickedness is this?'*

Then he wrapped the woman in his cloak, placed her upon his horse and galloped home.

FOR DAYS SHE LAY AS ONE DEAD. Sir Liontooth paced and the snow fell and the north wind howled. Skins and soft furs covered the woman. Fires burnt day and night to melt her ice. Candles blazed. Sir Liontooth refused to leave her side. Patient as a dog he fed her possets. His horse stood idle in the stable.

His old knights, neglected, grumbled and forgot him. His squires watched, said nothing, but wondered at some madness in his face which was not there before. At last she woke. She smiled and stretched like a child. Her eyes were the colour of violets. Sir Liontooth looked into them and was lost.

'My love,' he whispered. 'My only love.'

And the woman in her turn looked at Sir Liontooth and saw goodness enslaved.

THEY WERE MARRIED in the spring and from that day everything began to change.

'Bound to a rowan tree,' whispered the Witch Hazel. 'Why did he not see, why was he not warned? Her crime must have been most dreadful!'

'He is blind,' sighed the Witch Elm, 'blind and mad. And since the madness is of his own making, alas, we are powerless.'

So Lady Liontooth smiled and laughed her pretty tinkly laugh and opened

her violet eyes extremely wide. And Sir Liontooth walked by her side – from the first blue of the Morning Glory to the soft yellow lamps of the Evening Primrose – and thought himself the happiest of men.

DISCORD WORKS LIKE A MOLE, underground, out of sight, yet with powerful shoulders. The first victims of Lady Liontooth's trouble-making were the Ladies Fern and Tulip who watched over the wardrobe; their permission had to be asked before any article was removed. The following precious items were stored in the wardrobe of the harmonious garden: one Bishop's Hat, one Bear's Breeches, one Gardener's Garters, ten Bachelor's Buttons (yellow), six pairs Foxgloves, one Bridal Veil, two Lady's Mantles, one Lady's Smock, one Lady's Lace, four pairs Lady's Slippers and – last but not least – Granny's Bonnets. Waking from their winter sleep, the two old ladies had discovered that the Bridal Veil was missing. Dismayed, they reported its loss to Sir Liontooth.

'My love,' he asked his wife. *'Have you perchance seen a Bridal Veil?'*

'What? An old white thing with a greenish centre?' replied Lady Liontooth. *'Indeed I have and thrown it away. Did I do wrong, my heart?'* she cooed. *'It looked shabby and old-fashioned. Quite unworthy of a place in your wonderful garden.'*

Witch Hazel shook her yellow head. *'Now it begins,'* she muttered. *'Now it begins.'*

WORSE WAS TO COME. In the courtyard of the pink chateau stood the Bay Tree, wisest of Sir Liontooth's advisers. He was upright and venerable; and his sheltered position pleased him since cold winds did not. He was an old tree, given to speaking his mind in the council of trees. Lady Liontooth detested him.

'Our friend seems lonely,' she pouted one day. *'Shall we not move him onto the terrace, my love, nearer to the other trees? It has crossed my mind that a Trumpet Vine positioned against that sunny wall would fill his place to perfection. Why? It could play fanfares each time you depart and each time you return. That would be a fine thing would it not?'* And she opened her violet eyes extremely wide and stroked Sir Liontooth's arm.

So the Bay Tree was moved. That summer the winds blew cold and from the north-east. The old hate the wind. By autumn the Bay Tree's leaves were sadly burnt. By the following spring, although a distraught Sir Liontooth had laboured for months to save him, the old tree was dead.

Discord rejoiced and struck again. With a soft word here, a veiled threat there, Lady Liontooth turned plant against plant, tree against tree. Toad Lily was her spy, Fat Hen her confidante and spinner. Thick as butter

Grandville del   Imp.Delamain et Sarazin r. St le Cœur 8.Paris.   Ch. Geoffroy sc.

she spread her mistress's lies: Sir Liontooth had criticised the Creepers. Sir Liontooth had grumbled at the Grasses. Sir Liontooth thought the Dog Roses badly trained. Sir Liontooth declared the Enchanter spent too many hours asleep under his Nightshade. And so on and so forth.

The poison started to take effect. Sections of the garden became sulky and discontented. Feuds broke out. Grudges simmered like soup.

But Sir Liontooth, blinded by love, saw nothing. Others were not so blind:

'*Ssss. What poison she spreads,*' hissed Snake's Head.

'*Let me go to him. Now, before it is too late,*' growled Leopard's Bane.

The Witch Elm shook her branches. '*We must bide our time. Rowan-cursed her powers are great. Spells she turns against the spellers. Truth she twists against the tellers. We must bide our time.*'

The children, once so cheerful, stood miserably together.

'*Look,*' whispered Sweet Violet to Sweet William. '*The Willow is weeping.*'

One morning Sir Liontooth awoke to find a third of his garden gone. Distraught, he walked his land and saw the gaps; and each gap, each bare piece of earth, was a knife in his heart. There Wild Clematis had clambered, the Bramble borne its juicy fruits, the Grasses waved and wandered. Trees shivered, naked of their Ivies.

Banks, robbed of their Buttercups and Daisies, Celandines and Speedwells, stood empty. Fat Hen had flown, and with her, Henbit.

'Find me Gallant Soldier,' said Sir Liontooth to his squires. Then he looked into their faces and saw his command to be as empty as air. The children were crying.

'What is it, my dears?' asked Sir Liontooth. *'Robin has gone,'* they sobbed. *'Ragged Robin and Sticky Willie and Creeping Charlie. They went away and never said goodbye.'*

Sir Liontooth descended to the loving wilderness and found it a wasteland. He listened for the growl of Dog Rose in the Hawthorn and heard nothing. Butterflies fluttered, looking for Nettles.

Shepherd's Purse was missing, Canadian Fleabane nowhere to be seen.

Worst of all, the Enchanter had vanished.

'Treachery,' rumbled Giant Bellflower and shook his bells in disbelief.

Sir Liontooth shivered. *'There is no treachery,'* he said. *'Only my blindness.'*

A laugh tinkled from one of the turrets of the chateau. Sir Liontooth shivered again. Toad Lily would have brought the news to her mistress. Suddenly he felt the old hole in his heart. The two squires exchanged glances. Then Honesty spoke:

*'My lord, there is something else you must bear. The Yellow Archangel
is nowhere to be found.'*

Sir Liontooth turned as pale as death. He heard the clear voice saying:
*'Do not move the Bay Tree, Sire. Her ladyship's concern is not equalled by her
knowledge.'* He heard his own voice raised in anger. He saw the old tree dying
in the wind.

'Come, Sire,' whispered Sneezewort, *'come and rest.'*

Sir Liontooth stared like a madman at the grief of the Witches
and the distress of the Elders. There was bewilderment on Giant
Bellflower's face and in Widow Iris's eyes a terrible pity. It was
the last he could not bear. With a cry he ran from them, fled
into the grotto and crouched there, weeping as if his heart would break.

A YEAR HAD PASSED. It was September again. There now lived, just outside
the boundaries of the harmonious garden, a strange new community. It made its
own laws and had its own name – the Weeds. It hated, with a deep and
committed hatred, Sir Liontooth and all that he stood for.

Its leader was Fat Hen. Fat Hen had achieved power by the route known
to all ruthless and ambitious people and seldom patrolled by the good and
honourable. At first the exiles from the garden thought her simple and called her
Goosefoot. But she was an excellent listener – attentive, uncritical, full of soft

cluckings. She had a gift for flattery, knowing how often and how thickly to apply it. She had no heart, only envy in her downy green breast.

Methodically, meticulously, she had spilled anger into this ear, bitterness into that heart. She preyed on the Weeds' deep-rooted sense of injustice, fanning with eloquent cackles the embers of their hatred. Nettles began to sting. Woody Nightshade took the name Bittersweet and bore poisonous berries. Fox and Cubs changed their name to Orange Hawkweed. Sticky Willie called himself Cleavers, the Rosebay Willow-herb became Fireweed. As for Cow Parsnip who had never hurt a fly, she turned into Hogweed, a giant of 10-foot tall, who brought up blisters on any hand rash enough to touch him in sunlight. Even the Russian Vine became a tyrant. He called himself Mile-a-minute and smothered anyone who got in his way.

For one whole year Fat Hen had plotted how the Weeds might invade the harmonious garden and seize it for their own. Then heads would roll, prisoners be enslaved, leaders denounced. She and Lady Liontooth would begin a reign of terror most delicious and dreadful. Her hour, their hour, had almost arrived. Her wattles were black with glee.

One dark night Fat Hen called the Weeds together.

'Friends, outcasts, exiles!' she cried. *'I have a plan. A plan which will restore to us not only our dignity and our pride but also our rightful home.'*

A sighing and a rustling.

Fat Hen spoke again: *'Who drove us out? The Cruel Lion. Who let us go? Those who were our friends. What do we owe them?'* Fat Hen's cackle rose to a shriek: *'Nothing but hatred!'*

An answering roar swept over the Grasses, through the Creepers and into the Tubers, thick and baleful. Fat Hen crowed with pleasure. Behind her Cuckoo Pint, Henbit and Chickweed, her lieutenants, preened.

She spoke again – this time softly: *'Two nights before the new moon we shall attack and murder our enemies in their beds. Fireweed shall burn and Woundwort wound; Cleavers shall cut and Bramble slash; Nettle shall sting and Bindweed bind; Bittersweet poison them, Spear Thistle puncture them, Sowthistle trample them! Aark!'*

Unknown to Fat Hen, there was one weed, an unobtrusive thing, who still lived in the harmonious garden. She grew under the Indian Horse Chestnuts on the garden's boundary with the weedlands. She had no name.

If someone had told her to leave she might have left. But her roots were deep. And throughout her short life no-one had ever noticed her existence.

Except, that is, for one person. During the making of the harmonious garden, Sir Liontooth had come upon the flower

and noted with interest her ragged leaves and thick, coarse body. He had stroked her yellow head and smiled – and the flower had never forgotten his smile. Since then, largely ignored, she had become a catcher of sound, setting her clocks to the wind's faintest whisper. Now she, and she alone, had overheard Fat Hen's plan.

But what was she to do? The wilderness, the banks were deserted. No Horse Chestnut heard anything but the tossing of its mane.

'*I cannot warn him,*' thought the flower despairingly. She was rooted too deep to move. Just then Sir Liontooth's squires climbed the hill. A frown spoilt the friendly gap between Honesty's eyes. Sneezewort's bobbles had lost their bounce. They sat down in the grass only inches from the flower.

'*My lords . . .*'

Honesty looked at Sneezewort and Sneezewort looked at Honesty.

'*My lords . . .*'

The voice, slow and awkward, came from beneath their feet. Rising, the two squires saw the yellow head surrounded by its rosette of ragged leaves. They bowed low and the flower forgot she was ugly.

'*Speak, lady,*' smiled Sneezewort and she began. And as she told them what was to come, it seemed as if the harmonious garden fell silent – as a bird does, put from the light into a dark place.

In the great-walled vegetable garden Sir Liontooth was inspecting his

beans: the Broads with their black and white epaulettes, the French graceful as dancers, excitable beans from Italy and the English Runners – every inch cavalrymen, from their green breeches to their red tassels. Above this redoubtable army hung Apricots and White Peaches. In a corner Marrows, sleek as seals, basked in the autumn sunlight. Giant Bellflower saw Sir Liontooth's moving head and paused in his work. He searched in one of his bells and found his plan of what a vegetable garden should look like: neat rows of onions and carrots, neat rows of lettuce and cabbage, neat rows of potatoes and parsnips, neat rows of beetroot and radishes. He studied the plan wistfully, then put it away.

'*Whoever heard of a vegetable garden of beans?*' he mourned.

Honesty and Sneezewort ran out of the chateau and over the north drawbridge.

'*Where is our lord?*'

'*Among his beans . . .*' The old Giant peered at the squire: '*What ails you, Honesty? Your face is quite white.*'

But the boys were gone.

They found Sir Liontooth half asleep under a wall. He smiled up at them. Then his eyes narrowed.

'*What is it?*' Gently he shook Sneezewort's shoulder. '*Tell me, boy.*'

So they told him what the flower with no name had overheard –

how Fat Hen planned to invade the garden at dead of night and murder all in their beds; that Lady Liontooth and Toad Lily were a part of the evil conspiracy.

'Two nights before the new moon is the night before Michaelmas,' said Honesty. *'We have but seven days.'*

'Tell the company of the harmonious garden that I will address them this evening,' said Sir Liontooth. Then he closed his eyes.

The word was out, the news run like Fireweed round the garden.

'Who-who-who will lead us? Who-who-who will save us?' sobbed the woodpigeons.

Sir Liontooth awoke in the evening shadows. He left the great-walled vegetable garden, crossed the north drawbridge and climbed one of the chateau's pink turrets. At the top was a small door. He knocked on it.

'Is that you, Toad Lily?'

It was not a voice he knew. Sir Liontooth opened the door and walked into darkness rank and sweet. Something pale moved. No human form. A worm, monstrous, foul-smelling. He tore the curtains from the window. By the time he turned the worm had vanished.

Lady Liontooth, all innocence and virtue, greeted him with outstretched hands. Her eyes were very violet.

Grandville del.   Ch. Geoffroy sc.

'My love, you do me great honour!'

Sir Liontooth bowed coldly to his wife and took her by the wrist.

'We have business together, you and I,' he said.

One by one the Evening Primroses lit their lamps. An old moon climbed into the sky. The garden waited.

'He comes,' purred Panther Lily, who could see in the dark. *'And she is with him, our enemy the pale one. Why look! She trembles like Shaking Grass in the summer wind.'*

Sir Liontooth came out of the shadows holding his wife by the arm. Together they stood before the garden in the moonlight.

'On these counts we stand guilty,' he said. *'Of being evil and doing evil – her crime. Of bringing evil among you – my crime. Of harming that which I love – my crime. How do you judge us?'*

The Witch Elm, mightiest of trees, answered: *'The woman shall go back to the wood. We ask neither blood nor burning. You, Sire, are the beat of our heart. We are one.'*

And from the garden came a call so clear and sweet and true that Lady Liontooth covered her ears in terror and fled into the night.

Grandville del.   Ch. Geoffroy sc.

'We have but seven days, we have but seven days . . .'

Early next morning Sir Liontooth hurried to the bank where Old Bloody Warrior lived. Old Bloody Warrior was gruff as a bear and prickly as a hedgehog – but for valour in battle and placing of troops in the field he had no equal. Nor had he waited until now to consider the defence of the garden.

His plan was polished and ready, a fine strong harness waiting for its horse. He had been too clever for Toad Lily; too clever for Fat Hen who saw only a sleepy old man; too clever for Lady Liontooth who, if she had guessed his true nature, would have had him cut down years ago.

'Thou shall not tell the serpent by its skin,' hissed Snakeshead, swaying at Sir Liontooth's heel.

'Sire . . .' The red figure bowed deeply.

Sir Liontooth smiled. *'Speak, wiliest of commanders,'* he said.

Very soon Old Bloody Warrior's plan for the defence of the garden was known to every tree and plant. This is how it looked, copied out in fair hand by the Scholar Tree:

Plan for the defence of the Harmonious Garden

A line of sentries to guard the far south-east, south and south-west boundaries of the garden: the Indian Horse Chestnuts. Their orders are to stay where they are until the weeds have come past them and into the garden.

Two detachments of scouts: the Lamb's Ears. These are to be posted on either side of the lake. Their task is to monitor the Weeds' advance and send reports to the main force by Forget-Me-Nots working in pairs.

The first line of defence: a trench. This must be dug across the sloping ground between the lake and the chateau and the ponds above and below drained and left as booby traps. Both trench and ponds will contain Cupid's Darts and Sweet Rockets which, fired at close range, should cause alarm and despondency.

A

The second line of defence: foot soldiers. In their ranks are Snake's Head, Biting Stonecrop, Dogwood, Dog's ~~Tooth~~

Tooth Violets, Catmint, Monkey Flower and the Snap-dragons. Their job is to bite the roots of the enemy.

The third line of defence: the infantry led by Sir Liontooth armed with Kingspear. His troops consist of Honesty and Sneezewort (Sneezewort holding Sweet Flag), Old Bloody Warrior and his Soldiers and Sailors, the Broad, French and Italian regiments of beans, Mexican Sunflowers, Greek Varú

Greek Valerians, Hollyhocks, Morning Glorys, Japanese Anemones, Red Hot Pokers, Spearwort and Spearmint, Giant Bellflower, Dwarf Reedmace, ten Golden Clubs, ten Butcher's Brooms - and Trumpet Vine to sound the charge. They will fall on the enemy and cut them down..

On the wings: the cavalry, a strong force of Panther Lilies, Tiger Lilies, Foxtail Lilies, Leopard's Bane and the Runner Beans led by Zebra Rush. (Bear's Breeches to run messages between the wings.)

The defence of the chateau, the last stand, lies with the Witches Elm and Hazel, the Siberian Wallflowers, Hardy Plumbago, the Marvel of Peru, sixteen Broad Bucklers, sixteen Hard Shields and Giant Himalayan Cowslip. Flame Flowers and Chilean Fire Bushes must be stacked on every turret. (The very young and the old and frail will be sheltered inside the chateau.)

PART TWO:

the battle

In the grey light of dawn Sir Liontooth and Widow Iris walked among the Lilac. On the terraces below, Giant Bellflower, assisted by Dwarf Reedmace, was emptying the ponds. He had already dammed the stream in the Wild Cherry forest which fed them. Now he watched as their waters ran down to the lake, looking here, looking there, playing hide-and-seek among the reeds and sedges, ruffling the green cloak of the Water Hawthorn. Their abandoned dwellings became craters, turning the terraces into a moonscape.

'**Wot big 'oles!**' cackled Dwarf Reedmace. Giant Bellflower glowered at him: '**Shortwit, loon, mudhead! Be about your business and fill those holes with weapons.**' Then he stalked off, leaving his crestfallen assistant counting Darts and Rockets.

Snap-snap-snap-snap! The Snapdragons were demonstrating their jaw action to a Dogwood while the Dog's-tooth Violets squeaked and tumbled and bit each other's tails. Biting Stonecrop shook his yellow curls at them:

'**Foot soldiers you are not,**' he declared. '**Give me Dogwood as my comrade.**'

'**Well said,**' purred the Catmint, waving her tails. The Violets blushed with mortification. The Dogwood turned pink with pleasure.

'**How is my flower with no name?**' enquired Sir Liontooth.

He and Widow Iris had paused to watch the infantry drilling under the eye of Old Bloody Warrior.

'**She blooms,**' replied his companion. '**She is loved and respected and cannot quite believe it.**'

Some days before, on Sir Liontooth's orders, Giant Bellflower had gone with Dwarf Reedmace to the bank where the Indian Horse Chestnuts kept watch and the shy flower with the yellow head grew. Bowing low, he had told her of his lord's desire: that she, to whom they owed their lives if Fat Hen were defeated, should come and live among them and be honoured. Then, very carefully, he had lifted the portion of earth in which the flower was rooted and carried her high on his shoulder into the middle of the harmonious garden to a salute of Cathedral Bells and fanfare of Trumpet Creepers.

'I do not believe this,' thought the flower. *'It is a dream and soon I shall awake.'*

But she had not awoken. And now, a part of the harmony and lonely no longer, she saw that what had gone before had been the dream.

It was the blackest of midnights. No wind, no rain. No sound but for a dry slithering as, beneath the leafy caparison of the Indian Horse Chestnuts, the ground seemed to move and change shape. Fat Hen's soft-footed infiltrators were on the move.

Her revenge had begun.

Her plan of attack, although relying heavily on the element of surprise, had a military precision. She also possessed a secret weapon – poison! The Wartweeds with their bright green doublets and flat yellow heads looked innocent; but once their milky sap made contact with skin or eyes, it poisoned. The berries of the Bittersweet, red and tempting, were also fatal.

Fat Hen had positioned her poisoners strategically among the advancing wings of Dog and Stinging Nettles so that, when the moment came, they would fold together and paralyse the garden in their grip.

Her most terrible troops took up their battle formation at the centre: Fireweed the destroyer, Sowthistle and Swinecress, Spear Thistles, Brambles and Cleavers, the strangler Bindweeds, White Brionies, Japanese Knotweeds, Stinking Mayweeds, Woundworts and – most terrible of all – Giant Hogweed.

'If any awake and see him they will die of fright!' tittered Henbit.

Fat Hen shook her wattles: *'Patience, my baby bit,'* she crooned. *'Soon, when the soft-footed infiltrators send word that the garden sleeps, we shall advance; as the jungle moves and cannot be halted, as the tide sweeps in and cannot be turned.'* She remembered Gallant Soldier's insult and tore angrily at the grass. To have offered him command of her army and to have been rejected. She remembered the Enchanter's contempt, the cold eyes of the Yellow Archangel. Rage choked her. When victory was hers they would pay for their insolence.

Cuckoo Pint, pale green hood pulled close over his purple head, slithered down the boundary bank. **'They have reached the lake,'** he whispered. No serpent moved so silently, no worm so watchfully as Fat Hen's soft-footed infiltrators: Creeping Buttercup, Creeping Softgrass, Creeping Thistle, Creeping Cinquefoil, Creeping Yellowgrass, Ground Ivy, Ground Elder and Scutch, Squitch and Twitch, the couch grasses. White tentacles probing, they oozed through the soil.

They reached the lake and stopped, sniffing, listening. Water Hawthorn held her breath, Skunk Cabbage moved not a whisker, Kingcup hid his yellow head deep in his shiny leaves.

'All sleep, the way is clear, go back and tell the fat one,' hissed Squitch. Then he fastened his antennae onto a smooth rock.

Had he left his antennae free, he might have heard a Lamb's Ear prick. Like hares in November stubble the grey listeners caught the sound and received the message. At once they passed it to the Forget-me-nots who ran with it to Sir Liontooth and Old Bloody Warrior, hidden with their army on the terraces. On the wings the cavalry stood ready. Steam rose from the Snapdragons. The foot soldiers gritted their teeth. Even the Greek Valerians were silent.

'Are the Rockets and Darts primed?' whispered Sir Liontooth.

'They are, Sire.'

'They must not fire until the Weeds are upon them. Do they know that?'

'They know, Sire.'

Sneezewort cleared his throat. Hoping to stop his hands shaking he tightened his grip on Sweet Flag.

'Hold onto me, boy,' commanded a stiff old Butcher's Broom. **'It will ease me to know that a warrior guards my flank.'**

A warrior? Suddenly Sneezewort felt much better.

The Forget-me-nots reported in, the blue flowers on their caps quivering in excitement:

'My lord, the enemy is advancing!'

Across the valley a dark mass moved. A dull howl – a Wolfsbane looking for blood – hung in the night.

The battle of Fat Hen had begun.

When Sneezewort was an old man he sometimes tried to remember what happened on that terrible Michaelmas day, so confused, so dark in his mind, so long ago. Often a small hand tugged at his sleeve.

'Tell me how Fat Hen and the Weeds fell into the holes, Grandfather. How Giant Bellflower rescued Honesty. And what happened to Giant Hogweed . . . Please, Grandfather. Please tell!'

Memory, sluggish at first, moved. He could see shapes in the dark. Then he could see – O terror – hairy monsters rising from the lake, with hoods, long prickly arms, fronds curling and uncurling, swollen pods, six-foot spikes, greedy tentacles. Then he could hear . . . Crack! Whoomf! as the Sweet Rockets launched themselves from their craters . . . Ooh-aoh! Erk! Ooh-aoh! Friss! as divisions of Fat Hen's force fell into the empty ponds . . . Zig! Zig! as the Cupid's Darts hit their targets. Then a howling and roaring which burst his eardrums.

Cuckoo Pint, his hood torn from his head, blundered through the darkness. He struck out at something soft and fat, only to be seized by a beak. Fat Hen shook him like a worm.

'Poltroon! White liver!' she screeched. *'Go and tell the Bindweeds, the Black and the Hedge and the Small, to throw bridges across the craters. Send word to the poisoners to wheel in from the wings. Giant Hogweed, a dart in his side, runs amok. Let him run! His pain and fury will make him a thousand times more terrible. We may not murder them in their beds, Cuckoo Pint, but we shall win the night.'*

Sir Liontooth's foot soldiers had engaged the soft-footed infiltrators. Snap! Ground Ivy lost a bunch of her feelers. Trik! The Dog's-tooth Violets bit a Creeping Yellowcress clean in half. Monkey Flower, his crimson-scarlet coat bristling with rage, leapt on Scutch and tore off one of his long white feet. As for the Dogwood, he was everywhere – growling, barking, seizing great mouthfuls of Ground Elder and shaking it like a rat.

The two infantries met with a crash. Sneezewort saw Sowthistle charge. The creature with its piggy eyes was coming straight for him, tusks curved beneath the rootling snout. He froze – unable to move, unable to cry out. Then something flashed from Sir Liontooth's arm and the boar fell, King's Spear buried deep in his hairy side.

For hours the two armies struggled, backwards and forwards, backwards and forwards. Haar-ootah! Haar-ootah! The cries of the Japanese Anemones, slicing and whirling at the Japanese Knotweeds, rose above the clamour.

Now, slowly, the enemy showed its strength. The Bindweeds had sealed the craters with a close-matted covering, trapping the Sweet Rockets and Cupid's Darts, allowing Fat Hen's army to inch its way upwards, pulling plant and tree into its web. It ravaged the Runner Beans, brought down the Indian Horse Chestnuts, drove back even the bravest with its squirts of poison.

Dwarf Reedmace, a Golden Club clutched in his hand, dealt Stinking Mayweed such a blow that several of her heads fell off.

Sneezewort heard a shout, spun round and saw Cleavers coming for him. Could this be Sticky Willie, the boy he had once played with? The thing was upon him, its downward-pointing bristles ready to seize and smother. Sneezewort swung his Butcher's Broom . . .

Bravely the garden fought on. Then Bear's Breeches panted to Sir Liontooth's side, showing an unexpected turn of speed in one so portly:

'My lord,' he gasped. **'Leopard's Bane sends word the left wing cannot hold. It is the poisoners, my lord. They strike – and once the poison works, their victims cannot move . . .'**

'*Sound the retreat!*' called Sir Liontooth to Bugle. '*Tell everyone to fall back to the chateau and carry the wounded inside. Be of good heart. All is not lost.*'

He turned and touched Sneezewort on the shoulder. '*Courage is to know fear and conquer it. You, my dear, have enough for all of us.*'

Suddenly there was a scream of terror.

'*Help me! Oh, please help me!*'

Sneezewort fought his way through the mess of shapes and colours.

'*Honesty! Where are you, Honesty? Hold on! I'm coming!*'

He saw his friend. Honesty was caught in the tentacles of a Hedge Bindweed. The creature had wrapped him like a parcel, twining its stems round his thrashing arms and legs. Soon it would have him by the throat. Desperately Sneezewort tore at the tentacles, only to feel them whipping round his own body and fastening like limpets onto his back and thighs. As all seemed lost, two huge hands came down from the sky. They unpicked the rubbery ropes as if they had been threads of cotton.

'*That's a nasty thing, that is,*' rumbled Giant Bellflower. '*You ought to be more careful, young masters. You really ought to be more careful.*'

The pink chateau was now surrounded. Bindweeds and Ivies snaked across the moat. The Hollyhocks had their backs to the wall. One by one the Siberian Wallflowers were plucked from their embrasures by Giant Hogweed. Of the Morning Glories, later re-christened the Death and Glories because of their gallantry, not one remained.

Fat Hen scented victory: '*Storm the bridges!*' she screamed. '*Climb the battlements!*'

And the hairy hordes, encouraged by her shrieks, began to chant:

'*Fireweed shall burn and Woundwort shall wound*
Cleavers shall cut and Brambles shall slash . . .'

Fire came – but not from Fireweed. High in the turrets the Witches Elm and Hazel, helped by the children, flung down Flame Flowers and Chilean Fire Bushes upon the heads of the Weeds. There was panic. Even Giant Hogweed shrank back. Some Weeds jumped into the moat. Others burnt like bonfires. Suddenly the Witch Elm cocked her bushy head.

'**Listen,**' she cried. '**Do you hear it? A distant call out of the east?**'

Sir Liontooth heard it. Fat Hen heard it and knew fear. The flower with no name heard it and felt a great joy.

Into the garden swept the dawn and with it legions of colour, wave upon wave. The Yellow Archangel had kept his word, Gallant Soldier his faith. The Russian Vine was there, the Enchanter with his Nightshade, the Scarlet Pimpernel, the Poppies like drops of blood.

Sneezewort wiped the sweat from his eyes. He saw Hardy Plumbago and the Marvel of Peru dancing together in a turret.

'**We are saved,**' he stammered. '**Honesty! We are saved!**'

The light, the fire, the fury were too much for the Weeds. Surrounded on all sides they turned and fled. Sir Liontooth lifted King's Spear and drove it into Fat Hen's heart. The Trumpet Vine sounded a fanfare, the Bugle his glacier call.

The battle of Fat Hen was over.

EPILOGUE:

Dent-de-Lion

WHEN THE CHEERING HAD died down Sir Liontooth received his rescuers. First came the Yellow Archangel – to whom he gave leave to live in the shade of trees and spread his silver cloak through the orchards. Then came Gallant Soldier, homesick for the loving wilderness, followed by the Enchanter and his Nightshade, Ragged Robin (with even more holes in his pink jerkin) and the Fox and Cubs who squeaked and ran about, as out of control as ever.

Cow Parsley asked to live quietly on the boundary banks and her wish was granted. The Russian Vine wept quantities of tears. Sir Liontooth comforted him and said the old Apple tree where he had used to lie was waiting for him and that he was most welcome. Herb Robert and Mind Your Own Business came forward. The Scarlet Pimpernel was granted a sunny spot, the Dog Roses their leafy kennels by the lake, the Buttercups and Daisies their favourite banks.

Yellow Celandine, blood-red Poppy, blue Speedwell made their bows. Canadian Fleabane stood like a stork, his plumed seeds drifting about in the air.

'We have been much tormented during your absence,' observed Sir Liontooth, watching with relief as a long line of fleas left his property. *'Choose your nook or cranny.'*

The Rosebay Willow-herb hung back. *'I am ashamed,'* he muttered. *'I am Fireweed who has burnt you.'*

'It was I, not you, who started this fire,' said Sir Liontooth. *'And since the garden has forgiven me, how can I not forgive you and those other Weeds who came to save us? You are our beloved Willow-herb and shall spread your pink carpets where trees have fallen or where fire has cleaned the ground.'*

Then he turned to the plants and trees of the garden.

'I wish,' he said sadly, *'that every plant could be restored to its rightful place. Alas, it is not possible. Change is not a garment to be unpicked. Now certain of the Weeds will always be our enemies: the Brambles, the Bindweeds, the Hogweeds, the Nettles. Nor will the soft-footed infiltrators – the Ground Ivies, the Ground Elders, the Couch Grasses and the dwarfish Creeping Thistle – rest until they have overrun us. Cuckoo Pint, Chickweed and Plantain cannot change their ways . . .'*

'Sire!'

A square-stemmed fellow with a violet-blue head spoke up. It was Heal All with his red and yellow assistants, the Blanket Flowers.

'My lord, we have work to do. Great are the piles of Red Dead Nettles and White Dead Nettles. There are the wounded to be cared for – and Love-Lies-Bleeding. Let us begin and save what we can.'

Then Heal All, beloved of bees, went to work.

ALL WINTER LONG THE GARDEN SLEPT, its scars healing under the snow. One night when the north wind howled and whimpered the Witches brought Sir Liontooth news of his wife. She had been found lifeless in the wood, not a mark upon her body. He bowed his head and prayed for her soul although he feared she did not have one. The curse of the Rowan had been fulfilled. Nor was Toad Lily ever seen again.

SPRING CAME AND WITH IT, new life; and summer brought an event so noisy, so joyous, so rich in colour and pageantry that for centuries afterwards the oldest trees still talked of it.

One morning Sir Liontooth and Widow Iris were married under a white rose. Bishop's Hat conducted the service, the Yellow Archangel pronounced the blessing and the rose was named Wedding Day. Before the music and the revels Sir Liontooth called for silence.

'We owe our lives and our present happiness to a very gallant lady. You all know her. She is our guest of honour today and shall forever be remembered for her loyalty, her courage and her modest disposition.'

He turned to the bank beside the Lilac where a flower – quite an ordinary flower with ragged leaves and a yellow head – grew in the grass.

'Tell me,' he asked the flower. 'Have you a heart's desire?'

A hush fell upon the harmonious garden – a hush broken only by the

crooning of the woodpigeons and the drone of a solitary bee.

'*I would like a name,*' answered the flower.

Sir Liontooth gave her his sweetest smile. Then he faced the flowers and trees of the harmonious garden and said:

'*Because I owe this lady my life, I give my name – Liontooth – to her and to her kind for ever. But because she is gentle and feminine and Liontooth is a hard man's name, I shall give her the fairer French version which is Dent-de-Lion. She is the cause of my happiness today. So I decree that – in years to come – lovers shall play "she loves me, she loves me not"' with her gossamer clocks and so help to spread her seed wherever the careless wind may blow it.*'

AND THERE WE MUST LEAVE Sir Liontooth and Widow Iris and Giant Bellflower and the Witches Elm and Hazel and Honesty and Sneezewort and the Yellow Archangel and the Elders half-asleep in their parliament.

The centuries have passed. Cities have grown upon cities. Sir Liontooth and his heartbreak and the battle in the garden are only a dream dreamt long ago.

Just a dream. Except . . .

Can you think of a garden that doesn't have – in some small private corner of it – a ragged-leaved flower with a yellow head called a Dandelion?

postscript

Leontodon – Dens Leonis – Dent-de-Lion

DANDELION

Also called Blowball, Gowans, Dasheflower, Swine's Snout, Time-table, Wiggers and Priest's Crown.

THE DANDELION IS a medicinal herb, especially good at helping to cure liver and kidney disorders. It makes you pee (the French call it *Pissenlit*!), increases your appetite, and made into a tea relieves indigestion and dizziness. It is used in many patent medicines. Gipsies drink Dandelion Tea as a tonic to clear the skin and eyes. They also use the milky juice of the plant to remove warts. The Dandelion is not poisonous.

THE DANDELION GIVES a weather forecast. When it's a fine day all parts of its flowerhead are extended; but if the weather looks like rain the Dandelion's head closes up.

THE DANDELION HAS early opening and closing hours. Its flowerhead opens at 7am, depending on the intensity of the light. It closes at 5pm to protect itself against the dews of evening and stays shut all night.

THE DANDELION IS a honey-producer. In the early Spring, just when the bees have finished harvesting the blossoms of the fruit trees, the Dandelion gives out large quantities of pollen and nectar. Beekeepers love it because it flowers from Spring right through to late Autumn, long after most flowers have stopped blooming. Bees love it because Dandelion nectar is much more delicious than artificial bee food.

NO LESS THAN 93 different kinds of insects visit the Dandelion to drink its nectar.

DANDELIONS MAKE VERY good rabbit food. You can feed them to rabbits from April to September. Small birds love Dandelion seeds. Pigs chew up the whole plant, and so do goats. Horses won't; and sheep and cattle aren't too keen, although a feed of Dandelions is supposed to increase their milk yield.

THE ROASTED ROOTS of the Dandelion are used to make Dandelion Coffee which you can buy in most Health Food shops. Dandelion Coffee is said to be better for you than ordinary tea and coffee. It also won't keep you awake if you drink it last thing at night.

YOU CAN MAKE Dandelion Beer, Dandelion Soup, Dandelion Tea, Dandelion Wine, as well as delicious sandwiches and salads with young Dandelion leaves. (Always tear the leaves. This way they keep their flavour.)

DANDELION TEA

INFUSE ONE OUNCE of Dandelion flowers in a pint of boiling water for ten minutes. Strain, sweeten with honey, and drink several glasses during the day.

LES FLEURS ANIMÉES

SECONDE PARTIE

DE GONET ÉDITEUR

APPENDIX II:

plantings

BEAR'S BREECHES *(Acanthus sinosus)*
Flamboyant biennial which prefers well-drained soil but is not fussy. The hooded flowers are purple and white. Flowering time is summer. Height: 90-120 cm/3-4 ft.

BISHOP'S HAT *(Epimedium rubrum)*
Semi-evergreen hardy perennial which tolerates dry shade and prefers rich retentive loam. Red-tinted foliage. Red/yellow or white flowers. Flowering time is spring. Height: 30 cm/1 ft.

BITING STONECROP *(Sedum acre)*
Evergreen hardy perennial, happy on top of walls or among paving stones. Likes lots of sun and dry soil. Yellow flowers. Flowering time is all summer. Height: 5 cm/2 in.

BLANKET FLOWER *(Gaillardia 'Wirral flame')*
Hardy perennial which prefers chalky, well-drained soil and full sun. Deep red and gold flowers. Flowering time is summer to mid-autumn. Height: 75-90 cm/2.5-3 ft.

BROAD BUCKLER FERN *(Dryopteris dilatata)*
Hardy fern which likes dense shade and clay. Pretty arching leaves. Lasts from spring to autumn and dies down in winter. Height: 60-120 cm/2-4 ft.

BUGLE *(Ajuga reptans 'Atropurpurea')*
Evergreen creeping hardy perennial which likes its roots damp and full sun for best leaf colour. Deep blue flowers. Flowering time is late spring to early summer. Height: 10-15 cm/4-6 in.

BUTCHER'S BROOM *(Ruscus aculeatus)*
Evergreen hardy shrub which grows in any soil, shade or sun. Bright red berries in autumn if a female shrub is grown beside the male. Berry time is autumn to spring. Height: 60-90 cm/2-3 ft.

CATHEDRAL BELLS *(Cobaea scandens)*
Half-hardy climber which likes well-drained soil and a sheltered site. Grows very fast. Flowers are at first greenish white then deep purple. Flowering time is midsummer to mid-autumn. Height: 3-6 m/10-20 ft.

CHILEAN FIRE BUSH *(Embothrium coccineum lanceolatum 'Norquinco Valley')*
Slightly tender half-hardy tree, evergreen, which prefers a moist soil. Mild districts produce brilliant scarlet flowers. Flowering time is late spring to early summer. Height: 4.5-9 m/15-30 ft.

CHILEAN POTATO TREE *(Solanum crispum 'Glasnevin')*
Slightly tender, semi-evergreen scrambling shrub which likes a warm sheltered site and well-drained soil. Flowers are bluish purple and yellow. Flowering time is early summer to mid-autumn. Height: 4.5-6 m/15-20 ft.

CREEPING JENNY *(Lysimachia nummularia)*
Hardy evergreen perennial which likes damp shady places but also produces dense leafiness in drier soil and partial sun. Flowers are yellow. Flowering time is summer. Height: 2-5 cm/1-2 in.

CUPID'S DART *(Catananche caerulea)*
Hardy perennial which likes light, rather dry soil and full sun. Blue flowers, excellent for cutting. Flowering time is summer. Height: 60 cm/2 ft.

DOG'S-TOOTH VIOLET *(Erythronium dens-canis)*
Hardy bulb which thrives in the shade of deciduous trees and a humus-rich soil. Pinkish purple flowers. Flowering time is spring. Height: 10-15 cm/4-6 in.

DWARF REEDMACE *(Typha minima)*
Aquatic hardy perennial which likes to be planted in fertile mud under a few centimetres of water. Brown fruiting flower heads are short and fat. Flowering time is summer. Height: 30-60 cm/1-2 ft.

EVENING PRIMROSE *(Oenothera biennis)*
Hardy biennial which grows well in dry, infertile soil. Self-sows. Good ground cover. Yellow, sweet-smelling flowers opening in late afternoon. Flowering time is summer to mid-autumn. Height: 75-90 cm/2.5-3 ft.

FAIR MAIDS OF FRANCE *(Ranunculus aconitifolius flore pleno)*
Hardy perennial which likes a rich moist soil. Sunny position with a bit of shade. Double white flowers. Flowering time is late spring to early summer. Height: 45-60 cm/1.5-2 ft.

FAIRY MOSS *(Azolla caroliniana)*
Perennial which can be damaged by bad weather. Likes floating in shallow ponds in a mixture of sun and shade. Turns red in autumn, otherwise green. Height: 2-5 cm/1-2 in.

FOX AND CUBS *(Hieracium aurantiacum)*
Hardy perennial which is happy in sun or shade and any soil. Flowers are bright orange. Flowering time is all through the summer. Height: 15-30 cm/6-12 in.

FRENCH MARIGOLD *(Tagetes patula)*
Half-hardy annual introduced to the UK in 1573. Likes lots of sun, not fussy about soil. Flowers are golden yellow and maroon. Flowering time is summer to mid-autumn. Height: 30 cm/1 ft.

GARDENER'S GARTERS *(Phalaris arundinacea 'Picta')*
Hardy perennial grass which likes a damp soil. Spreads fast if given room. Creamy green and purplish leaves variegated with cream. Flowering time is early summer. Height: 90-150 cm/3-5 ft.

GIANT BELLFLOWER *(Campanula latifolia)*
Hardy perennial, happiest among trees where the soil is rich and well-drained. White or blue flowers. Flowering time is mid summer. Height: 95-120 cm/3-4 ft.

GRANNY'S BONNETS *(Aquilegia)*
Hardy perennial, also called Columbine, which doesn't mind sun or shade but dislikes dry soil. Blue, soft pink and purple flowers. Flowering time is late spring to early summer. Height: 60 cm/2 ft.

GREEK VALERIAN *(Polemonium Caeruleum)*
Hardy perennial which likes a rich damp soil and plenty of sun. Flowers are blue or white, leaves feathery. Flowering time is late spring to mid summer. Height: 60 cm/2 ft.

HARDY PLUMBAGO *(Ceratostigma plumbaginoides)*
Slightly tender spreading perennial with colourful autumn foliage. Needs full sun and light, well-drained soil. Deep blue flowers. Flowering time is midsummer to autumn. Height: 23-30 cm/9-12 in.

HONESTY *(Lunaria annua)*
Hardy biennial which likes a well-drained chalky soil. Tolerates shade. Flowers are lilac-purple, seed pods silvery. Flowering time is late spring to midsummer. Height: 75 cm/2.5 ft.

JAPANESE ANEMONE *(Anemone hybrida)*
Hardy ground-covering perennial which prefers a substantial moisture-retentive soil. Also grows but flowers less in full shade. White flowers. Flowering time is late summer to mid autumn. Height: 90-105 cm/3-3.5 ft.

KING'S SPEAR *(Asphodeline lutea)*
Hardy perennial which likes a well-drained soil, full sun or a sheltered site. Sweetly scented yellow flowers. Flowering time is summer. Height: 90 cm/3 ft.

LAMB'S EAR *(Stachys lanata)*
Evergreen hardy perennial which likes chalk and hot dry soil. Soft and furry foliage, mat-forming. Purple flowers. Flowering time is mid summer. Height: 30-45 cm/1-1.5 ft.

LEOPARD'S BANE *(Doronicum plantagineum)*
Hardy perennial which likes a heavyish moisture-retentive soil. Large yellow flowers pale in strong sun. Flowering time is mid-spring to early summer. Height: 75 cm/2.5 ft.

LOVE-LIES-BLEEDING *(Amaranthus caudatus)*
Hardy annual which needs rich soil, full sun and shelter. Popular for cutting and dries well. Crimson flowers. Flowering time is midsummer to early autumn. Height: 75-90 cm/2.5-3 ft.

MARVEL OF PERU *(Mirabilis jalapa)*
Half-hardy annual needing rich soil in a warm sheltered site. Flowers are a mix of yellow, red, white and pink and heavily scented. Flowering time is midsummer to early autumn. Height: 60-90 cm/2-3 ft.

MEXICAN SUNFLOWER *(Tithonia rotundifolia 'Torch')*
Half-hardy annual which grows quickly in rich, well-drained soils and sheltered sites. Orange/scarlet and yellow flowers. Flowering time is midsummer to mid-autumn. Height: 1.2 m/4 ft.

MONKEY FLOWER *(Mimulus cupreus)*
Moist soil near pools or streams suit this hardy perennial. Needs dividing frequently or to be grown from seed each year. Crimson-scarlet flowers. Flowering time is summer to early autumn. Height: 15 cm/6 in.

MORNING GLORY *(Opomoea rubro-caerulea)*
Half-hardy annual climber which likes full sun and a light, fertile soil. Plant in a warm, sheltered position. Beautiful sky-blue flowers. Flowering time is midsummer to early autumn. Height: 2.4-3 m/8-10 ft.

PANTHER LILY *(Lilium pardalinum)*
Hardy bulb, easy to manage in light shade and a spongy mixture of loam, leaf-mould and sand. Orange and orange-yellow flowers. Flowering time is midsummer. Height: 1.5-2.1 m/5-7 ft.

RED HOT POKER *(Kniphofia)*
Slightly tender perennial which must have good drainage, warmth and full sun. Red and yellow flowers. Flowering time is midsummer to early autumn. Height: 1.05-1.2 m/3.5-4 ft.

RUSSIAN VINE *(Polygonum baldschuanicum)*
Hardy climber which can be planted in any soil. Established specimens grow over 4.5 m/15 ft in a season. Useful for covering sheds, dead trees etc. Flowers are white. Flowering time is midsummer to early autumn. Height: 12-15 m/40-50 ft.

SIBERIAN WALLFLOWER *(Cheiranthus allionii 'Golden Bedder')*
Hardy biennial which likes chalk and hot dry soil. Spicily fragrant deep yellow flowers. Needs full sun. Flowering time is spring to early summer. Height: 40 cm/15 in.

SNAKE'S HEAD *(Fritillaria meleagris)*
Hardy bulb which prefers clay and is happy in short grass where there is moisture. Purple and white bell-shaped flowers. Flowering time is spring. Height: 30-45 cm/1-1.5 ft.

SNEEZEWORT *(Achillea ptarmica 'the pearl')*
Hardy perennial which likes chalk and hot dry soils. Flowers are bright white bobbles. Flowering time is midsummer to early autumn. Height: 60-75 cm/2-2.5 ft.

SWEET BAY *(Laurus nobilis)*
Evergreen shrub, slightly tender with aromatic foliage. Needs frequent trimming if planted in tubs. Can also be allowed to grow freely. Susceptible to burning in cold winds. Height as shrub: 1.5-1.8 m/5-6ft.

SWEET ROCKET *(Hesperis matronalis 'Mixed')*
Hardy perennial but best treated as biennial. Loves moist alkaline soil and sun/shade. White, purple and lilac flowers, fragrant in the evening. Flowering time is late spring to midsummer. Height: 60-75 cm/2-2.5 ft.

SWEET WILLIAM *(Dianthus barbatus)*
Hardy biennial which likes chalk and full sun. Flowers are mixed – red, pink and white with a slight, clove-like scent. Flowering time is summer. Height: 45-60 cm/1.5-2 ft.

TOADFLAX *(Linaria purpurea 'Canon J. Went')*
Hardy perennial which likes a light, hot dry soil. Will seed itself and stay true. Pink flowers. Flowering time is midsummer to early autumn. Height: 79-90 cm/2.5-3 ft.

TOAD LILY *(Tricyrtis stolonifera)*
Hardy perennial which thrives in shady peaty places but needs warmth. Delicate purple-spotted flowers. Flowering time is late summer to mid-autumn. Height: 60 cm/2 ft.

TRUMPET VINE *(Campsis radicans)*
Slightly tender climber which needs a really warm site, full sun and rich soil. Aerial roots on stems cling to the surface of walls. Orange and red flowers. Flowering time is late summer to early autumn. Height: 12 m/40 ft.

WIDOW IRIS *(Hermodactylus tuberosus)*
Hardy tuber which thrives in sharply drained, chalky soil. Flowers are olive green and black. Flowering time is spring. Height: 30-40 cm/12-15 in.

YELLOW ARCHANGEL *(Lamium galeobdolon 'variegatum')*
Hardy perennial, very vigorous in fertile, moisture-retentive soil. Likes dense shade, can spread well over 240 cm/8 ft wide. Yellow flowers on white-marked leaves. Flowering time is early summer. Height: 30 cm/1 ft.

APPENDIX III:

glossary

GLOSSARY

't' in Liontooth title – Widow Iris
Publisher's info – Common Dog's-tooth Violet
Author's note – Chequered Fritillaria
Dedication – Yellow Amaryllis
Page 1 – Golden-flowered Currant
Page 2 – Narcissus
Page 4 – Lilac
Page 5 – *left:* Bear's Grape, *right:* Foreign Dragon's-head
Page 6 – Marvel of Peru
Page 7 – *left:* Star Anemone, *right:* Large Blue Greek Valerian
Page 8 – Bay
Page 9 – *left:* Changeable Iris, *right:* Hairy-leaved Toadflax
Page 10 – 'Queen Marguerite'
Page 11 – *left:* Peach-leaved Bellflower, *right:* Pygmy Water Lily
Page 12 – Sweet Pea
Page 13 – *left:* Heart-leaved Magnolia, *right:* Deadly Nightshade
Page 14 – Dahlia
Page 15 – *left:* Canadian Dogwood, *right:* Pretty Larkspur
Page 16 – Pansy
Page 17 – *left:* Black-eyed Susan, *right:* French Marigold
Page 18 – Cactus
Page 20 – Peach Blossom
Page 21 – *left:* Christmas Rose, *right:* Common Passion Flower
Page 22 – Lily
Page 23 – *left:* Sweet-scented Tulip, *right:* Tree Violet
Page 24 – Tulip
Page 25 – *left:* Pea-formed Bitter Vetch, *right:* Fraser's Evening Primrose
Page 26 – Primrose and Snowdrop
Page 27 – *top right:* China Pink, *bottom right:* Hybrid Loose-strife
Page 28 – Hemlock
Page 29 – *left:* Spiniest Scotch Rose, *right:* Leopard-Spotted Slipperwort
Page 30 – Violet
Page 31 – *left:* Clustered Bellflower, *right:* Common Henbane
Page 32 – Nasturtium
Page 33 – *left:* Four-angled Andromeda, *right:* Characias Spurge
Page 34 – Hawthorn

Grandville del.   Delamain et Sarazin, Imp. r Col le

GLOSSARY

Page 35 – *left:* Broad-leaved Willow-herb, *right:* Bitter Sweet
Page 36 – Thistle
Page 37 – *left:* Tuberous Indian Cress, *right:* Three-Leaved Arum
Page 38 – Water Lily
Page 39 – *left:* Italian Bugloss, *right:* Honesty-leaved Phlomis
Page 40 – Jasmine
Page 41 – *left:* White Zephyranthes, *right:* Sad Larkspur
Page 42 – Water Shoot
Page 43 – *left:* Tiger-Spotted Lily, *right:* Forget-Me-Not
Page 44 – Wall Flower
Page 45 – *left:* Virginian Lungwort, *right:* Panicled Lungwort
Page 46 – Poppy
Page 47 – *left:* Rose of Sharon, *right:* Splendid Catchfly
Page 66 – Marvel of Peru, Myrtle and Tobacco
Page 68 – Daisy
Page 69 – *left:* Japan Apple-Tree, *right:* Indian Chrysanthemum
Page 70 – Mourning Bride and Marigold
Page 71 – *left:* Scarlet Bladder Senna, *right:* Great-flowered Self-heal
Page 72 – 'The Return of the Flowers'
Page 73 – *left:* Lobed Peony, *right:* Party-coloured Lupin
Page 74 – Rose
Page 75 – *left:* Virginian Spiderwort, *top right:* Tiger Flower, *bottom right:* Three-coloured Lachenalia
Page 76 – Dandelion
Page 80 – 'The Animated Flowers'
Page 88 – Forget-Me-Not
Page 90 – Honeysuckle
Page 92 – Cornflower and Poppy
Page 94 – Grape Vine

COVER ILLUSTRATION –

Flowers: Lamb's Ears, Cupid's Darts, Sweet Rocket, Snap Dragons, Japanese Anemones, Honesty, Mexican Sunflowers, Hollyhocks, Red Hot Pokers, Giant Bellflower, Runner Beans, Zebra Rush, Broad Buckler Ferns, Indian Horse Chestnuts

Weeds: Stinging Nettles, Giant Hogweed, Fat Hen, Toad Lily, Bindweed, Bramble, Sowthistle, Cleavers, Japanese Knotweed, Bitter Sweet, Cuckoo Pint, Creeping Thistle, Creeping Buttercup, Rosebay Willow-herb

A LINE OF SENTRIES to guard the far south-east, south and south-west boundaries of the garden: the Indian Horse Chestnuts. Their orders are to stay where they are until the Weeds have come past them and into the garden.

TWO DETACHMENTS OF SCOUTS: the Lamb's Ears. These are to be posted on either side of the lake. Their task is to monitor the Weeds' advance and send reports to the main force by Forget-me-nots working in pairs.

THE FIRST LINE OF DEFENCE: a trench. This must be dug across the sloping ground between the lake and the chateau, and the ponds above and below drained and left as booby traps. Both trench and ponds will contain Cupid's Darts and Sweet Rockets which, fired at close range, should cause alarm and despondency.

THE SECOND LINE OF DEFENCE: foot soldiers. In their ranks are Snake's Head, Biting Stonecrop, Dogwood, Dog's-tooth Violets, Catmint, Monkey Flower and the Snapdragons. Their job is to bite the roots of the enemy.

THE THIRD LINE OF DEFENCE: the infantry led by Sir Liontooth armed with King's Spear. His troops consist of Honesty and Sneezewort (Sneezewort holding Sweet Flag), Old Bloody Warrior and his Soldiers and Sailors, the Broad, French and Italian regiments of beans, Mexican Sunflowers, Greek Valerians, Hollyhocks, Morning Glories, Japanese Anemones, Red Hot Pokers, Spearwort and Spearmint, Giant Bellflower, Dwarf Reedmace, ten Golden Clubs, ten Butcher's Brooms – and Trumpet Vine to sound the charge. They will fall on the enemy and cut them down.

ON THE WINGS: the cavalry, a strong force of Panther Lilies, Tiger Lilies, Foxtail Lilies, Leopard's Bane and the Runner Beans led by Zebra Rush. (Bear's Breeches to run messages between the wings.)

THE DEFENCE OF THE CHATEAU, the last stand, lies with the Witches Elm and Hazel, the Siberian Wallflowers, Hardy Plumbago, the Marvel of Peru, sixteen Broad Bucklers, sixteen Hard Shields and Giant Himalayan Cowslip. Flame Flowers and Chilean Fire Bushes must be stacked in every turret. (The very young and the old and frail will be sheltered inside the chateau.)